This story was born out of the intergenerational love, strength, and power that Indigenous people have passed down for generations. In my life I have been blessed to have experienced and witnessed Indigenous love, and there is no love as fierce as that of a mothers. I've spent my life surrounded by matriarchs; grandmothers, aunties, cousins, friends, and future matriarchs too. I watch as they pass down our languages, our laughter, our recipes, and our way of loving.

There have been times when Indigenous parenting was deemed less than, when their gifts were no longer allowed to be passed down, but instead replaced with anger, hate, and violence. In my lifetime I have seen our gifts return and our intergenerational brilliance and love thrive once more.

Together, we are raising Warriors. Warriors who walk steadily in their moccasins and who walk with love in their hearts. They are coming for all that their ancestors were denied.

This book is for all the Indigenous parents and caregivers who are learning to let go of anger and instead plants seeds of love and power. To all of the parents and caregivers reclaiming Indigenous love and kinship; and to all of the babies coming into a world that once sought your destruction, your existence alone shows our ferocity.

Dear little Ogichidaa; You are loved. You are sacred.

Willie Poll

Little Ogichidaa, my wish for you... _____

_____

_____

_____

_____

_____

_____

_____

_____

                                    _____

Dedications

Willie Poll

This story came to me after watching Raven Lacerte, the co-founder of the Moose Hide Campaign, speak to thousands on the Campaign's Day of Action to end gender-based violence. She stood there with a future matriarch, her baby girl, on her hip, while also glowing and soon to be bringing new life earth side. There are often moments where I think of the challenges Indigenous people have and continue to face and I radiate with anger, but watching her, the only thing I felt was love and power. Her and her family taught me that true social change will come from love; and I have been beyond blessed to have felt that love from many of the Lacerte matriarchs; and more so, have witnessed the change it is making across Turtle Island.

To learn more about The Moose Hide Campaign and the moose hide pins worn on page 21-22 visit their website at www.moosehidecampaign.ca

Hawlii Pichette

To all the new mothers being born in the tender moments, as they hold their babies with honour and a depth of love they have never felt before.

My Little Ogichidaa

An Indigenous Lullaby

Willie Poll

Hawlii Pichette

My little Ogichidaa, I can feel you grow
You carry more strength than you'll ever know

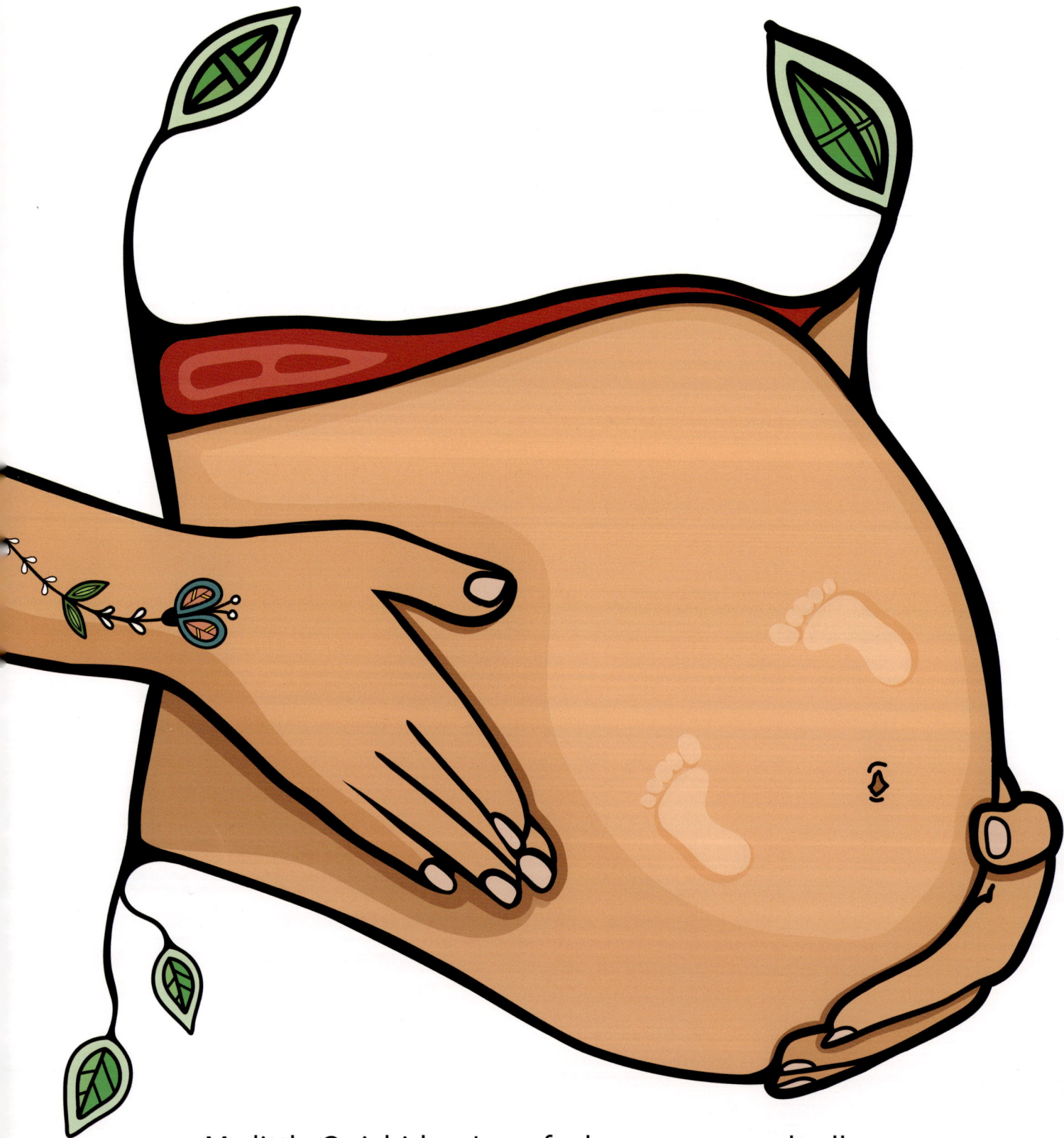

My little Ogichidaa, I can feel you move and roll
Little signs of the resilience you already hold

My little Ogichidaa, your future is bright
You carry with you our ancestors' fight

My little Ogichidaa, you will bring change
You will help release our anger and rage

My little Ogichidaa, you will break cycles
Your love will spread for miles and miles

My little Ogichidaa, you will be a truth seeker
My little Ogichidaa, you will be a big dreamer

You were a seed they did not mean to plant
You will grow so wildly, no one will ever tell you, "you can't"

Our language will flow through all of your being
And you'll never be silenced simply for speaking

The prayers of our ancestors have brought you to me
And once you are earth side, an Ogichidaa you will be

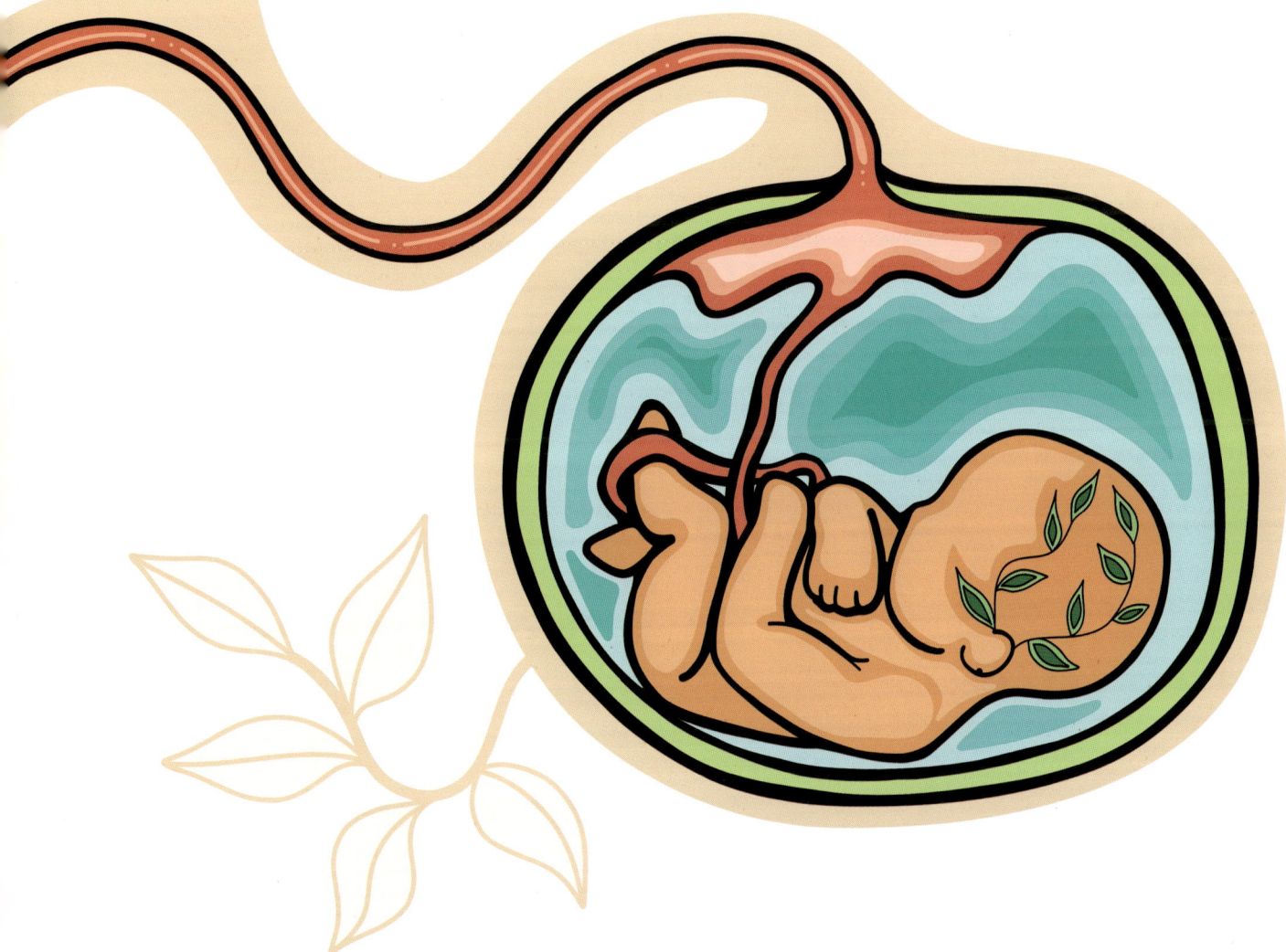

My little Ogichidaa, I know you will move mountains and you will make waves
You'll carry our culture, language, and love for all of those babies
in all of those graves

My little Ogichidaa, you're a medicine all your own
You are so loved that you will never be alone

My little Ogichidaa, you will protect all that is sacred
The plants, the animals, the water — we are all related

You bring hope to all our relations that live on this earth
With a promise of love and life, they will rejoice at your birth

My little Ogichidaa who lives inside of my womb
The tiniest seed they never expected to bloom

Coming into a world that sought your destruction
A thousand spirits behind you bringing disruption

My little Ogichidaa, with a fire in your eyes
Shining brighter than all the stars in all the skies

My little Ogichidaa, you will have passion that burns from your heart
You'll pick medicines, you'll dance, and you'll make beautiful art

My little Ogichidaa, my heart knows you will live free
One day you'll carry more knowledge, love, and culture than me

My little Ogichidaa, with the women, girls, and two-spirit you will stand
And many will join you to find the truth our people demand

My little Ogichidaa, your existence is a blessing
For it is their colonization your being is upsetting

My little Ogichidaa, take up your space
Because you and our people belong in this place

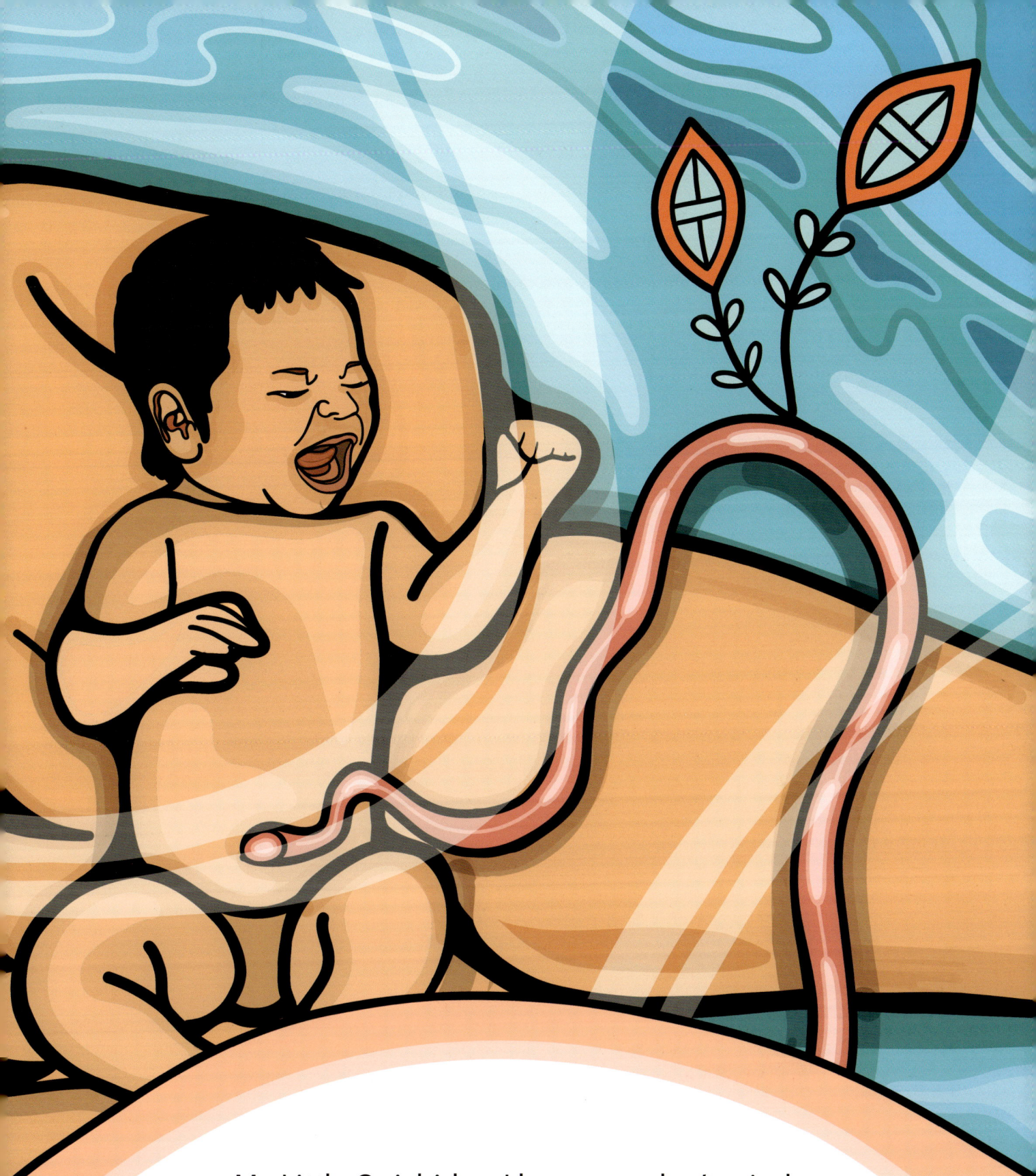

My Little Ogichidaa, I hope you don't mind
I borrowed some strength as I brought you earth side

I watched as you started to open your eyes
I listened to your first of many loud cries

I look at you and love washes over me
My little Ogichidaa, a great Warrior you will be

Willie Poll is a Métis author from the Robinson Huron Treaty Territory (Sault Ste. Marie, Ontario, Canada) and a proud member of the Métis Nation of Ontario. She holds a Bachelor of Arts in Indigenous Studies and a Master of Arts in Archaeology. She grew up with a close relationship to her Métis grandpa who filled her with stories that connected her to her ancestors and culture. Willie has worked in Indigenous education across the Nation for over 10 years. Her stories are her feelings, emotions, and her tribute to the youth in her life. Willie currently resides on Prince Edward Island as a guest on the traditional lands of the Wabanaki and Mi'kma'ki people; however, she lives a nomadic lifestyle and has had the opportunity to be a guest in many places across Turtle Island.

Hawlii Pichette of Urban Iskwew is a Mushkego Cree (Fort Albany FN, Treaty 9) urban mixed-blood artist and illustrator who currently resides in London ON. Born and raised in the small community of Cochrane, located in northeastern Ontario, her work is deeply influenced by her culture, upbringing, and reflects the beautiful interconnections of the natural world. Her practice includes illustrations, digital artwork, paintings and murals. She graduated from Fanshawe College's advanced Fine Art program with Honors in 2017, receiving the Satellite Award exhibition. She is also known for a series of Indigenous coloring pages that she illustrates and shares on her website.

Editor: Lisa Frenette
ISBN: 9781778540301
For more book information go to https://medicinewheelpublishing.com
Printed in PRC
We acknowledge the support of the Canada Council for the Arts.
Published in Canada by Medicine Wheel Publishing.

Medicine Wheel Publishing

Canada Council Conseil des arts
for the Arts du Canada

Funded by the   Financé par le
Government   gouvernement
of Canada   du Canada   Canada